I wish to dedicate this book to the memory of my late parents, Jean and Eric Perkins, who did so much for me in my formative years.

Margaret Jean Taylor

MY WORLD IN RHYME

AUSTIN MACAULEY
PUBLISHERS LTD.

A CIP catalogue record for this title is available from the British Library.

ISBN 9781786129000 (Paperback)
ISBN 9781786129017 (Hardback)
ISBN 9781786129024 (E-Book)
www.austinmacauley.com

First Published (2016)
Austin Macauley Publishers Ltd.
25 Canada Square
Canary Wharf
London
E14 5LQ

My grateful thanks are due to my husband, Freddie, who has helped and encouraged me in so many ways, too numerous to list here.

This book of my rhymes consists of some deeply held reflections, thoughts, emotions and reactions to life's events as I have experienced them and which might be of interest to others who may have shared some of those wide ranging experiences or who may discover companion emotions of their own.

Some of the poems reflect the world around me as I see it and my existence within it. I also pay tribute to some of those people who have influenced my life.

A number of the poems are expressed in a humorous vein whilst others are of a more serious and even a more philosophical nature.

The lengths of the rhymes vary considerably since a number are immediately reactive to circumstances emotionally affecting me, whilst others, perhaps those of somewhat greater length, have been the result of events and experiences that have provoked a more analytical chain of thought and emotion.

Margaret Taylor

CONTENTS

REFLECTIONS	**15**
FRIENDSHIP	**16**
OLD AGE	**17**
MY DREAM	**18**
NAMES	**19**
A CHRISTMAS MESSAGE	**20**
THE MIRACLE	**22**
NATURE'S COLOURS	**23**
SMILE	**24**
LIFE'S A JIG-SAW	**25**
ANGEL GUIDES	**26**
WHAT BIRDS ARE WE?	**27**
ANGELS	**28**
POLITICS	**29**
PRAYER	**30**
WHAT AM I?	**31**
THE GAMBLING MAN	**32**
LONG LOST FRIEND	**33**
MY LOVE	**34**
ONE SHATTERED LEFT ARM	**35**
THE HERB GARDEN	**36**
FAITH	**37**
THE FIRE	**38**
A LOAF OF BREAD	**39**
BRITAIN'S GOT TALENT	**40**
LOVE IS DEEP	**41**
MEMORIES KEEP YOU CLOSE	**42**
WATERWAYS	**43**

THE SALE	**44**
ANGELS	**45**
YOGA	**46**
OH, DREAM OF MINE	**47**
RACE AGAINST TIME	**48**
OSTEOPOROSIS	**50**
TRUE FRIENDSHIP	**51**
MY CAT, NAMED REESES, SADLY MISSED	**52**
VALENTINE ODE	**54**
MEMORIES OF A HOLIDAY IN ROME	**55**
LOVE	**56**
GOODBYE, WORLD	**57**
HOME	**58**
FORGIVEN	**59**
WAR AND PEACE	**60**
SIXTY YEARS	**61**
THOUGHTS OF MY LATE MOTHER, FROM ABROAD (CHILE)	**62**
WORD POWER	**63**
THE VISITOR	**64**
MOISTURE	**65**
SIBLING LOVE	**66**
BRIDGE	**67**
PICKLED	**68**
ODE TO RICHARD TANSLEY	**69**
BRIAN	**70**
A MORTAL SIN	**71**
THE PAST	**72**
POLITICAL SCANDAL	**73**
TO ROY	**74**
FOREVER	**75**
TO MUM AND DAD	**76**

AN ODE TO JOHN FINCH 77
THE INNOCENCE OF A HAPPY CHILD 78
ALL SUMMER RAIN 79
SPECIAL THOUGHTS FOR OUR BROKEN HEROES AT HEADINGLY GRANGE MILITARY REHABILITATION CENTRE, SURREY 80
THE MOON'S BEAM 81
MY HEART 82
YOUR JOURNEY 83
TWO WISE OWLS 84
FATHER TIME 85
THE LONELY WIDOW 87
GUCCI, MY CAT 88
A PRAYER 89
BELOVED 90
GEOLOGY 91
MY HUSBAND 92
THANK YOU FOR SHARING MY WORLD 93

Reflections

Looking back upon your life
Seems just a flash of time.
Some memories are filled with strife,
Or happiness sublime.

Innocence, then common sense -
Such wisdom comes with age.
And friends you make along the way
Who helped you with each stage.

Those toys you loved, that doll or train;
Those seaside trips that were such fun;
Electric storms and all that rain -
Such lovely memories every one.

Your life is like a special book,
Reflections that you'll measure.
Take time to ponder, then to look.
Fond memories to treasure.

Friendship

An unexpected friendship
Can blossom like a flower.
Its fragrance grows much sweeter
With an enigmatic power.

With time you share a troubled thought
When wrong decisions making.
Some comfort, then, you can have brought,
With wisdom undertaking.

As years pass on your friendship grows;
It's filled with love and laughter,
And like a sparkling stream it flows
To happily ever after.

The world seems such a nicer place
When love invades this empty space.

Its power to inspire.

Old Age

Invisible could be the word
When growing very old.
Though you'd dismiss it as absurd,
This tale must be told.

Was pushed and jostled in the town,
As young folks staring with a frown.
He struggled, moving extra quick
While clinging to his walking stick.

Wears his glasses – he can't see
When reading paper, or TV.
Then he'll have a little nap
But can't get up. Oh, double drat!

When eating supper all he'll get
Are gastric juices all upset.
Poor old body full of pain –
His joints are groaning yet again.

He sees the Doc to get some pills.
Surely these will cure all ills.
But coloured pills that he's been sold
Are just no cure for growing old.

A life of toil, mishaps and fun.
On his last day the angels come.
They'll end his old age misery
And take him to eternity.

My Dream

Whilst wandering through the land of dreams
Of waterfalls and forest streams,
A tiny path came into view -
I saw an image there of you.

Drawn as I was through fern and bracken,
Impediments along the way.
Shards of light displayed the beauty -
'Twas the dawning of the day.

The birds aroused me with their song,
Melodic in their glorious throng,
A wondrous sound of nature's making.
Then, I knew my undertaking -
Ever more to keep you near…

Your presence now forever dear.

Names

If there is no identity
Then surely its non-entity?
Everything must have a name
And no two names should be the same.

Names for dogs and names for cats;
For cars and clothes and silly hats;
Towns and streets and countries too;
Birds and creatures in the zoo.

Zap for scrubbing all your pans;
'Fairy' soap for washing hands;
Shelves of items in the store,
They cover every name and chore.

Liners, ships and tiny craft -
They wave "Ahoy!" as they sail past.
Posh named yachts with sails that quiver;
Narrow boats glide down the river.

But best of all on stage and screen,
To entertain they must be seen.
Those famous names – they are our stars
We cheer and clap with our "Hurrahs".

A Christmas Message

Peace on Earth – goodwill to men.
Shall we bomb Hanoi again?

At Christmas time the church bells ring
And happy children carols sing.
Then home to bed to dream away
Of Santa riding on his sleigh
To bring them toys in paper gay.

Jingle bells and mistletoe
Love thy brother – kill thy foe!

Yuletide log burns in the grate -
A family time to celebrate.
To eat and drink and eat some more,
Whilst friends come knocking at the door.
All are rich and none are poor!

Snowflakes falling from the sky -
Another thousand soldiers die!

A gift to you – a gift for me.
The fairy on the Christmas tree.
Paper chains adorn the wall.
Balloons are hanging in the hall.
A happy time is had by all.

Now is the season of good cheer,
Yet countless men still walk in fear!

God above – if God there be -
Look down on us and when you see
The way we celebrate this day
Do not turn your face away,
But grant us time to learn and pray.

Peace on Earth – goodwill to men.
Shall we bomb Hanoi again?

The Miracle

I want to go where love is,
That's where I want to be.
To fill my life inside and out.
I'm sure that's what it's all about,
That's how I came to be.

So now my world is only white,
Never to look back.
Decisions that are positive,
As negative is black.

WOW! Now I've found where love is.
It's not a lonely place.
Such beauty found in nature
Can partly fill this space.

I feel the greatest part of all
Is extra special when you fall.
When heavens open up above -
The miracle: "YOU ARE IN LOVE".

Nature's Colours

Blue, the colour that paints the sky.
Lush green, the grass where we can lie.
Grey are the clouds that gather round
When rain come pouring on the ground.
The yellow sun comes peeping through,
Then colours shine of every hue.
A rainbow sparkles in the sky,
With brilliant colours does supply
An arc of wonder from above.
A present from the sky with love.

Smile

You're smiling at a stranger;
You talk of this and that.
When making a connection,
It turns into a chat.

The conversation flows so well, so much you have to share.
A broken heart you help to mend,
Aware you have become a friend,
She offers you a chair.

The kettle boils – a cup of tea.
It follows from your sympathy.
How wonderful when friends can share
Some loving words to heal despair.

So reach out to a stranger, bring sunshine to their life.
And make them smile
Just for a while.
You'll ease away their strife.

Life's a Jig-saw

I consider life a jig-saw,
Each piece about a time.
When you complete the picture,
Then I'll create the rhyme.

There has to be a house somewhere -
A place you call your home;
In countryside or bustling town,
Where 'ere you choose to roam.

When pieces slot together,
They may be quite profound.
When life has stormy patches,
The pieces will confound.

Some times are complicated.
Wherever does it fit?
You search and search and then you'll find
That special little bit.

So many pieces make the whole;
Each person has their story,
And with your very last breath comes
Your final piece – and glory!

Angel Guides

We slot into our way of life.
It's natural that we do.
Then, opportunities arise
To change both me and you.
We alter our perception:
Sometimes see just one direction.
If only we could see between
And take away the strife.
For always there are many paths
And choices by the score.
Go forward with a loving heart -
And you will want no more.

What Birds Are We?

My legs are long but I'm quite pink
And rather elegant I think.
I'm really quite a clever dude
Through wading water, I find food.

With chest of red I look a treat.
My nest is always kept quite neat.
I live my life in garden fair.
Look closely and you'll find me there.

My coat is vibrant yellow;
It never seems to age.
I sing the sweetest little song
Through bars around my cage.

I swoop and dip high in the air
And deftly land with so much flair.
When summer's done I emigrate
To warmer climes. That is my fate.

From mountain cliff, on crags I stand
Surveying all the wondrous land.
When prey I seek with sharpened beak,
I swiftly swoop to catch my meat.

Angels

There are many angel helpers.
We have our spirit guide.
When special help is needed
With us they will abide.

In troubled times and sadness,
Or body full of pain,
Just pray to them, with gladness,
To turn life round again.

Beloved angels come to me
When times come that I cease to be.
Raise me up to place of rest.
With heavenly wings fulfil my quest.

Politics

Politics are quite taboo
When friendships you are making.
Opinions, that are clear to you,
To them may be mistaken.

Exposing who are greedy;
Support for poor and needy;
War torn countries everywhere
They need support to show we care.

The problem's surely human kind.
Of this we can consider.
We hope intelligence to find
In government of every kind.

We vote them to deliver!

Prayer

When sun is shining up above
And you are feeling low,
Just fill your mind with thoughts of love
To others you'll bestow.

Some folks have such bad luck
With finance and with health.
A thoughtful word or kindly deed
May help them when they are in need
And feeling very low.

That special gift to guide you
Is faith along the way.
The greatest problems can be met
Just realise you mustn't fret.
Dear God teach us to pray

What Am I?

A lick and a stick is all it takes
To send me on my way.
Nobody thinks of little me –
By aeroplane or land or sea.
To who knows where? That's where I'll be!

Either way they've had to pay.
It's not too much a bother.
A cheery letter or a card -
Sweet message to a lover.

So don't forget to get in touch
Your thoughtful greetings mean so much.

Buy a Postage Stamp!

The Gambling Man

The Gambling Man was dressed in black;
On trouble then he turned his back.
He had no conscience, that is clear,
On hurting them who held him dear.

He took their prize possessions
And sold them at the fair.
How could he be so cruel
To say he didn't care.

The money was to gamble
With chips he had to buy.
He hoped to scoop a million,
But plans just went awry.

He put a hundred chips on black -
A bitter sigh – there's no way back.
On red he should have put his stake.
That was his terrible mistake.

He's standing in the dock now.
The Judge has called him in.
And rowdy crowds were calling,
Making such a din.

The jury said they were displeased
With evil tales of his misdeed.
To gaol now sent – just for a bet!
Let's hope his gamble he'll regret.

Long Lost Friend

What happened to that childhood friend?
I loved him long ago.
Playing footie in the park;
Scrumping apples for a lark
And sledging in the snow.

I still recall that scruffy dog
When Mum left him in charge.
But Rover had a different plan.
With barking frenzy chased a van
And bounded off at large.

Our lives were always such a muddle -
Always in and out of trouble.
Teenage years with spots on face -
That crush you had on girl named Grace.

I wonder how your life turned out
I'm technophilic now.
'Friends Re-united' is my plan;
I'm hoping that your name I'll scan.
We'll meet again somehow.

My Love

"My love is like a red, red rose"
A poet wrote of old.
But my love's nothing like a rose,
Or anything so cold.

With untold joy and happiness,
And eyes like sparkling wine;
He's everything that I desire –
And, best of all, he's mine.

One Shattered Left Arm

The sun was shining, I recall.
The beauty of full spring -
Flowers in abundance
And the birds were on the wing.

I'd just popped out to catch the post
But dallied then to make the most.
This morning was a perfect host.
Walking on, I heard a lark
And sauntered on to Woodthorpe Park.

Then all of a sudden my foot slipped up and I slipped down
And I lay bereft upon the ground.
A doggy walker sauntered past.
My painful cries were heard at last.
That kindly girl gave me protection,
Walking in the same direction.

An ambulance then saved the day.
To hospital we sped away.
The pain was bad, so long it lasted,
But soon the nurses got me plastered.

It taught me quite a lesson
When I had that nasty fall.
If I take too much for granted
That memory I recall!

The Herb Garden

When you're in need of healing,
This message is revealing.
You'll find a herb of every kind
To heal the flesh and soothe the mind.

From ancient times and by-gone days
They've been applied in many ways.
Lavender is soporific –
With coughs and colds, it is terrific.
Thyme is a healer and sage a revealer

Patchouli is a sensual flower -
Tremendous scent with sexual power.
Geranium, the Ladies' herb
For treating hormones that disturb.
Sir Basil helps improve the mind,
When concentrating, you will find.

But fragrance, sweet, when all is done
The rose is still my favoured one!

Faith

Can beauty that was yesterday still linger on tomorrow?
A sunset glow,
Sweet flowers that grow,
A loving word with one who shared your happiness and
sorrow.

With faith, a new horizon: when thoughts of what was lost.
The stormy sea of life has calmed amidst the crags and
rocks.
The passing of the old year will refresh your hopes anew
And the sunshine that's tomorrow will now come into
view.

The Fire

When house had started blazing
They heard the family shout,
And fire brigade was on its way
To put the fire out.

Black smoke started pouring
From underneath the floor,
But firemen put the ladder up
To reach the second floor.

The braveness of the men that day
Was a tremendous feat,
And safely to the ground convey.
It made the family weep.

It was a faulty gas main
That caused that fateful fire.
So go and get your boiler checked
Or else you could expire.

A Loaf of Bread

Policemen then broke down the door
And found her lying on the floor.
Lack of nourishment they said
Was the reason why she's dead.

Gathering neighbours sobbed her name
And sought to allocate the blame.
But you who nodded when she passed,
When was it that you saw her last?

It must be several weeks or more,
Yet none came knocking at her door
To ask her health or lend a hand,
Her loneliness to understand.

You did not wish to interfere?
There must be some who loved her dear!
If they won't bother, why should you?
Well, yes! That is a point of view.

It seems so pointless that she's dead
Because she lacked a loaf of bread!

Britain's Got Talent

Britain's got talent and don't we have fun
Watching the amateurs' acts one by one.
Sometimes we are cheering contestants, or scorn,
With chronic embarrassment as they perform.
The high TV ratings are quite a relief,
'Cos public excitement is beyond belief.
As we long for the winner, the audience shout.
One by one they are falling – let's just vote 'em out!
That great act, Diversity, just won the day.
Simon Cowell is happy. It all went his way.

Ha! Ha!

Love is Deep

Enduring love in textured wrought
Sustains the passing years.
Some times may pass without a thought,
When disillusioned – overwrought.
Then loving thoughts creep into view
Reminding me that I love you.

Memories Keep You Close

Memories of your smiling face
Are with me every day.
I treasure them with all my heart
Since you have gone away.

The empty space you've left behind
No-one can ever fill,
For it belongs to only you
And it always will.

The sweet sound of your laughter
I hear once in a while.
It echoes in my head
And brings a little smile.

For since you have been taken
To pleasant pastures new,
My heart clings to each memory
That I hold, my love, of you.

Your sparkling eyes, your sweetness,
Your special little ways,
Are thoughts so poignant I recall
To help the longest days.

Waterways

Gaily painted narrow boat
Chugging on its way
With not a jot of urgency
To mar a lazy day.

Blue skies above, canal below
And gentle summer breeze –
Gliding so majestically
Beneath the leafy trees.

Drowsing at the tiller
Under cloudless sky
The old man feels contentment
As fields go drifting by.

Brightly coloured butterflies
Dance for his delight
And a line of tiny yellow ducks
Paddle into sight.

Sunlight warms the scented air
And meadow larks give voice.
What other way to spend the day
Given but the choice?

The Sale

Elevate and press the button.
Let's go in the lift.
The sale is on the second floor
And it cannot be missed.

On advertising it was cheap;
We rushed along to have a peep.
But disappointed as can be -
The model, there, we couldn't see.

The salesman said we were mistaken;
Fridge we wanted had been taken.
What a waste of time for sure
That journey to the second floor.

Angels

Where angels dare their wings unfold,
With messages impart,
Open your thoughts – their helping hand
Will heal your troubled heart.

Let your mind be open
With wisdom from above
And receive their information
For it comes with peace and love.

There are many angel helpers
With different tasks to do.
Their healing love will guide us -
They're God's gift to me and you.

Yoga

Here we lay in sweet repose.
Stretch your legs and bend your toes.
Let go – and have a meditation!

Calm your body, then your mind,
Soothing all, you just unwind.
Let go – and have a meditation!

Cobra, camel, shoulder-stand;
Control the breath and you should land.
Let go – and have a meditation!

Learn to love it and it should
Improve your health and you'll feel good.
Let go – and have a meditation!

Oh, Dream of Mine

Oh, dream of mine, dream on.
Let hopeful longing not be gone.
Encircle all that's treasured dear.
Encapsulate to hold it near – closer to me.
Protect and help the journey onward.
Vain hope for ever held in anticipation
Of happiness too long sought.
What price can it be bought?

Race Against Time

Tensed behind the steering wheel,
His senses filled with power.
The aim to get there quicker
And save just half an hour.

His heart, it was a-pounding
As he urged his motor on.
With eyes fixed on the road ahead –
Another mile post gone.

All other cars a challenge
As he raced past every one,
Hurtling down the motorway
Like a bullet from a gun.

The scenery fled backwards,
As foot pushed to the floor
And exhilaration mounted –
Urging motor to do more.

When suddenly the car ahead
Pulled out to overtake
And a stifled scream escaped him
As he stood hard on the brake.

The wreckage was strewn far afield
Of what was once his pride
And pieces of both car and man
Were pushed on to one side.

No more to race against the clock,
Manipulating gears.
He never did save half an hour –
He just lost thirty years.

Osteoporosis

Osteoporosis is fatally corrosive.
It burrows holes into your bone,
Making them crumble.
Then you'll have a tumble.

And plastered up they'll send you home.

A weak fractured bone
Is the cause of much pain.
So diet and exercise will be your gain.
A calcium drink with vitamin D,
Next followed by magnesium.
Though it is a tedium.

But guaranteed proven – you'll see!

True Friendship

True friendship is a Gordian knot
That angel's hands have tied,
And by its skill, their texture wrought.
Who shall its folds divide?

My Cat, Named Reeses, Sadly Missed

We used to play with strings and things.
You'd catch a ping-pong ball
And grasp it with your little paws.
You showed no fear at all.

A coat so thick and lustrous,
My little boy so strong.
You entertained me daily
With purr, meow and song.

I trained you with a whistle
And up the path you ran
It was your morning breakfast call.
(Last night's adventures did enthral)
Now here's your tuna can.

There was a very special friend
We called her Auntie Clare.
She knew your special little meow
To tell her you were there.

With constant store of special treats
And comfy bed to lie on.
More luck than this you couldn't beat.
You had the life of Ryan!

My darling, darling Reeses
Now I've to say goodbye,
And endless tears roll down my cheeks.
My love will never die!

You were my precious little friend
With sparkling eyes so bright.
So brave and valiant to the end,
My saviour of the night!

For nine long, loving years
You shared a life with me.
My grief is painful, little friend.
So sorry that it had to end when Angels came for thee.

Valentine Ode

Though we're in our twilight years I know I shall remain
Forever a romantic – that never seems to wain.
And so, upon St. Valentine's, this message I'll impart:
I hope you'll be forever near
To have good times and fill with cheer
This very loving heart.

Memories of a Holiday in Rome

We found the Trevi fountain.
Such beauty to behold.
Like water from a mountain,
Its sparkling furls unfold.
So many glorious buildings from ancient Roman city.
With narrow streets from Spanish Steps. But, here begins
my ditty!

The clouds unleashed a showery squall
And soaked us through, as I recall.
If only I had packed my mack,
But too late now to think of that.
The next plan was to find a cab -
And, dripping wet, we were so glad.

That taxi at the Coliseum
Saved us from the mausoleum.
We could have caught a deathly chill.
So "Goodbye Rome" – we've had our fill!

Love

A twinkling eye –
A gentle sigh.
That's what love is!

A poignant song,
Remembered long.
That's what love is!

A long caress.
A hug to bless.
That's what love is!

And throughout life with all its strife.
With blessings too, to help us through.
Its love that helps us to survive!

Goodbye, World

I have wings. I have wings.
Let me fly, oh, so high
Over treetops and houses,
Smiling down from the sky.

Many lands shall I visit,
Vast oceans, so deep,
With forests and rivers,
Wide canyons and creeks.

Cars look like ants, now,
Long highways they crawl
And masses of people.
Can God see them all?

I'll float to a place
That I've not seen before,
Where light is so wondrous.
What bliss to explore!

When I see all my loved ones,
I'm on the right track.
It will all be so perfect
I'll never come back.

Home

A bungalow in Brixton; a house on Hampstead Heath;
A cottage down in Oxford; a maisonette in Neath;
A two-roomed flat in Folkestone; a love-nest down in
Looe;
A stately home in London; a tent in Timbuktu;
A cave on Terra Ferma; a castle in the Air.
Any one should I call home – if you, my love, were there.

Forgiven

My life was slipping fast away;
No centre core was there,
Although I was surrounded
By loving friends who care.

But now I feel forgiven
For love has come at last.
A second chance I'm given;
No sad thoughts of the past.

I'll melt into your loving arms;
This wager I must trust.
For Cupid's arrow straight and true
Has pierced my heart with love for you.

War and Peace

When war clouds threatened England
He joined up with the rest
And trained and fought beside us
And really gave his best.
One couldn't fault his keenness
For he kept our spirits high
With jokes and songs and stories
When the bullets, they did fly.
Called friend by each and everyone,
Though they knew him not, before.
A brave and honest soldier
Who helped to win the war.

But when it was all over
And back to Blighty came,
He's standing in the job queues.
They never called his name!
Not wanted as a neighbour,
Not wanted as a friend,
Slighted by old comrades –
He wished his life could end.
In time of need they welcomed him,
But now they turn their back.
But yet he has not changed at all –
His skin is still as black.

Sixty Years

This is a very special year.
For Queen and country let us cheer.
Because our Glorious Majesty
Will celebrate her jubilee.

The torch has travelled through the land
To claim Olympic glory. And
Through all the challenges she's seen,
She has remained our glorious Queen

For Britain and for Commonwealth
Her duty was to gain our wealth.
For six decades she's been our guide
And long with us may she abide.

Thoughts of My Late Mother, From Abroad (Chile)

What do you think I ought to do?
There's cooking, washing, ironing too.
Fretting and planning – such dashing around,
My buzzing head – with plans abound.

This and that and then the other -
Send a birthday card to my mother.
Oh! But now there's no address….
Some lovely flowers will sure impress.

My love – next to her photograph:
She'll see their beauty and then she'll laugh.
How thoughtful, dear, how very kind!
Be peaceful now and calm your mind.

For healing can and will take place.
Your life will then be filled with grace.
Let slip away the hurt you're feeling
And your life will have new meaning.

Feel the beauty everywhere, and with
Your friends you too can share.
Take one small thought each day of life
To fill with joy – and not with strife.

Word Power

'Erudite' – it's so absurd.
It really is the strangest word.
This crossword's found me in a mess.
To seek it out I must confess
I'll pick the brains of Alan G.
Intelligence must be the key

To this one!

Alas, to see my word powers failing.
To Alan, though, it's just plain sailing.
The dictionary is 'wot' I need
To study hard and then I'll read.
Enlighten and improve my mind,
The answers then I'll surely find.

The next time!

The Visitor

(To Nottingham City Hospital)
Cool morning mist and palest sun
Put lyrics in my mind.
Transporting pen to paper -
Was best option I could find.
So, lovely friend, may I divulge
What's really in my heart?
The visits you have made each day
Have been the greatest part
Of my return to health and life,
And, hopefully, thereafter
So truly shall we both enjoy
Good times, with fun and laughter.

Moisture

Moisture is transported
In so many different ways.
It gushes down the drain-pipes
And in the gutter plays.

Moisture forms in droplets
From grey clouds up above,
Bringing precious water.
It's a blessing sent with love.

Moisture fills our eyes sometimes,
To overcome emotion.
The tears spill down upon our cheeks
Displaying our devotion.

Moisture can be white sometimes
When skies are full of snow.
It can be fun for winter sports
But makes the traffic slow.

Moisture feeds the Earth with life.
It came to give us birth.
So let us thank the water
For this our glorious Earth.

Sibling Love

My sister came to visit me.
It was a special treat.
Her train sped to the station,
That's where we were to meet.

She helped to sort my problems out.
We always have such fun.
Laughing lots and crying too,
Until our time was done

We went to find the Lincoln Imp.
Met friends for a Thai meal.
I did her face, she chopped my hair.
Much better did we feel!

Our lives are very different,
Yet we share our thoughts and love.
She is my dearest sister
Come down from heaven above.

Bridge

To bridge that gap it's great to find
A hobby to improve the mind.
A pack of cards lay on the table.
The challenge now – would I be able?
Patient teacher, where was he?
The U3A could be for me.
The tricks are key to winning all
And if you fail your contracts fall.
Sometimes I'm simply just not good -
Old age has turned my brain to wood.
Perseverance is the key
To master this – and then I'll see
This hobby really has my calling
Though at times I am appalling.
Ace and King, then Queen and Jack -
These are the masters of the pack.
But in the end, if I must fall,
My Queen of Diamonds has it all.

Pickled

My father was called Eric Perkins.
He was ever so fond of small gherkins.
One day for a spree
He ate ninety-three
And pickled his internal workings.

Just joking Dad!

Ode to Richard Tansley

How sad I am and full of pain
I'll never hear your voice again.
Fond memories are all that's left.
Why do I feel so bereft?

You were such a special person,
Kind and loving as a friend.
I pray we'll meet again in Heaven
When my days come to an end.

Passed away Sunday October 26th 2008.

Brian

He went in for a check-up
For the coughing fits he had.
I thought it sounded serious.
The doctor thought it bad!

He went up for an X-ray
Was told the very next day,
"No going home, it's far too bad.
You're staying in, right now, my lad".

Now, hospital is not a place
Where Brian had thought he had a space.
His heart was needing some repair
And so the surgeons kept him there.

When opened up, they did their best
To resurrect his ailing chest.
The nursing staff and all the team
Did sterling work – it was supreme.

The boring part that lay ahead -
To convalesce and stay in bed.
His family showed how much they'd care:
Transported homeward in despair

The one thing Brian couldn't claim
Was patience to be well again.
"So take it easy and you'll learn
That slowly good health will return".

A Mortal Sin

Adam's in the Bible.
He takes a wife called Eve.
But they commit a mortal sin
And practise to deceive.

It wasn't just an apple,
But the principle that counts.
When choosing good or evil,
Make sure what it's about.

The Past

Let's put the past behind us,
It's better that we do.
Forget the broken promises;
The years of memories, too.

The sunrise of the New Year
Will signify a start.
Let this be the beginning
And may we never part.

We'll share the days together,
Enjoying things we do.
New memories to treasure
Between us, me and you.

Political Scandal

The national press has had a ball
And one-by-one those MP's fall.
Expenses claims that were a farce;
A mole exposed their crooked path.

The Labour Party's had its day
And Gordon's very bitter.
Mandy's cunning business plans
Have brought him to a twitter.

Now Cameron has set the scene,
But their misdeeds are just obscene!
We're in a terrible dilemma -
This voting farce is just a never
Ending gravy train.

Till the next election then!?

To Roy

Pray thee come into my mind.
A happy thought you'll be.
I'll see your twinkling eyes again
And share a memory.

The fun we've shared together
While travelling round the Globe:
The cruise ships lights were sparkling.
The Caribbean glowed.

The mysteries of Egypt;
Corsica's golden shores;
The magic that is Disney
And many, many more.

A treasure trove of journeys.
There's so much to discover.
If health sustains, all that remains
Is home time – to recover.

Forever

Another age, another tear.
The passing of another year.
Dust is where they say we'll be,
But surely there's eternity.

How can it all be just for naught,
The endless battles that we fought.
When love and hate ran side-by-side.
To choose the right and then decide!

My Angel Guide please stay with me
And take me to eternity.

To Mum and Dad

I'm feeling sad and missing Dad
And Mum, I miss you too.
To have you here, I'd give so much
And feel again your tender touch.
I really did love you.

Memories are so poignant
Did we really share so much?
So many years of hopes and tears;
You had great wisdom and I fear
I listened not enough.

Please forgive my selfishness.
You sacrificed for me;
Daily toiled from dawn to dusk,
Helping me to be.

You gave me independence
And taught me to be strong,
But so often it was difficult -
My decisions were all wrong.

Now I'm a grandmother
And I love my children so.
How blessed my life in every way.
I'm so lucky – don't I know.

An Ode to John Finch

Meticulous, meticulous – are these lines ridiculous?
Not if you're creating a brand new place.
Each section is perfection,
The ultimate perception
Of minimal and stainless steel and lots of space.

Where can I find the master
Who'll create this masterpiece?
Perhaps I know already, this personage might be.
A bird in flight – come down to earth
And hear his sorry song of mirth.
Too-wit-too-woo! (Me!)

Expectation, realisation, disappointed as can be -
How can he be so hard of hearing,
Sitting in his pretty tree?
Methinks I'll draw my own creation,
Starting with a firm foundation.

Bold and bright and filled with grace,
I'll fill this very lonely space -
Well, almost!

The Innocence of a Happy Child

When Mummy reads the paper
She heaves a dreadful sigh.
There are photographs of soldiers
Oh! Daddy, did they die?

He said they did their duty,
Whatever that may mean,
And died for Queen and country.
Mummy said it was obscene.

So glad I'm not a grown up.
What's TV news about?
There's crowds of people shouting -
It's a riot there's no doubt.

Green issues and black people,
Unlike programmes that I see,
Which are made for little people.
Lots of fun and so happy.

Adventures in my story books
Are wonderful to read.
My loving home and Mum and Dad
Are all I really need.

All Summer Rain

It seems our country's drowning.
Of water there's no end.
Its downpour after downpour.
The heavens just descend.

For all the thousands homeless,
Their lives filled with despair,
Clearing up the slush and mud,
I say a little prayer.

I pray for all those people
Whose lives are torn apart.
Where, oh! where, is Noah
To build another Ark

Don't be afraid to try something new…
An amateur built Noah's Ark -
A professional built Titanic.
So what does that tell you?

Special Thoughts for Our Broken Heroes at Headingly Grange Military Rehabilitation Centre, Surrey

The light was fading fast away
To end another winter's day.
From frosty morning crisp and bright
Our task each day to help the plight
Of brave young men, now in our care,
Their injured bodies to repair.

Courageous soldiers to the end,
The Taliban have tried to bend
And break their courage, but no way!
With precious limbs they've had to pay -
These guys will learn to walk again
With prosthetic limbs that cause such pain

But worse than this, the sights they've seen
Remain with them, from where they've been.
For bombs and carnage filled the air.
We read the papers with despair.
Terrorists, such evil men,
Destroy, destruct and kill again.

If only we could live in peace.
An end to war that brings such grief
Dear God. Please hear us when we pray -
For our brave soldiers every day.

The Moon's Beam

I'm swinging on the Moon's beam
And drifting silently.
It's travelling through the Milky Way,
Stars sparkling in between.

I'm going to make three wishes.
The first I will divulge -
To send a million kisses,
Your sweet lips to indulge.

The others are a secret
Which someday I'll share with thee.
But darling heart, you know so well -
Mischief and mystery
I never could resist at all.
And so together we must fall
In perfect harmony!

My Heart

How you captured my heart?
Then indifferently shifted so smart.
Sad longing becomes expansive
Exploding in a tear.

The sorrow, the longing
Like a trembling leaf floats away on a gentle breeze
To be captured no more,
But fades away into a poignant memory
Of trifled emotions.

Your Journey

Your journey has been difficult,
But you've arrived today.
With courage, grace and fortitude,
It's here you need to stay.

Your future is looking brighter
As you put the past behind.
The love that's in your heart, right now,
Is what you sought to find.

Go forward with your Angel Guide;
Your footsteps will be lighter.
That sparkling smile you must not hide
Will see the World much brighter.

In nature you'll find happiness -
God's gifts sent from above.
The greenest leaf, the prettiest flower,
Will fill your life with love.

Two Wise Owls

Two wise owls sat in their tree.
First was he and then came she.
The moonlit sky was dark above
And twinkling stars declared their love.

The forest is the darkest place,
But those two loved this lonely space,
For they had wisdom from above.
And into view there came a dove!

She blessed them both, upon her way.
In forest dark she came to play -
No fighting wars of human kind -
With playful thoughts upon her mind.

They were as happy as can be
Sitting in their pretty tree.

Father Time

Time and tide wait for no man, that is true to say.
Weeks turn into months and years as minutes tick away.

The babe that's parents pride and joy
Will challenge all they have to give
On every outing – time and toy,
And hurtful deeds that they'll forgive.

With youthful zest the children grown -
Their next decision to leave home.
Young man with an enterprise
Starts a business in supplies.

Girls have dreams of a career.
Achievements come without a fear.
They earn some money have some fun,
Then marry when that time is done

The working man whose toil and strife
Has served the family all his life -
Let's hope the plans on his retiring
Have good years before expiring.

The lovely lady once so fair
With made-up face and stylish hair -
Now lined and wrinkled she will find.
The mirror can be most unkind!

So, after all is said and done,
Make sure those moments, everyone,

Are remembered with compassion -
And enjoy the latest fashion!

The Lonely Widow

Some folks spend and some folks save,
Dispensing it upon their grave.
When lawyer came to read her will,
Those greedy kind
Will have in mind.
But patience – just be still!

The kindness of that lady
Hasn't left her wealth to them,
But helping those without a home.
No longer would they have to roam
To start their lives again.

The lawyer shocked those folks that day.
No selfish gain had gone their way.
That lonely soul when laid to rest –
Her legacy was her bequest.

No need for house where she has gone,
Her spirit lifted higher.
No loneliness to dwell upon -
She's now become a flyer!

Gucci, My Cat

He prowls the garden when its night,
To tease the mice is his delight.
His feral instincts are his fun
When daily naps and food are done.

His fur is lustrous and he's wise
When studying – his sparkling eyes!
He loves to have a lot of fuss,
And after all, he is my puss.

A good companion sure is he,
But fur gets on my best settee.
A dog is fun and very fine,
But best of all this cat is mine!

A Prayer

When sun is shining up above
And you are feeling low,
Just fill your mind with thought of love
To others you'll bestow.

Some folks have such bad luck
With finance and with health.
A thoughtful word or kindly deed
May help them when they are in need.

That special gift to guide you
Is faith along the way.
The greatest problems can be met -
Just realise you mustn't fret.

Dear God teach us how to pray!

Beloved

I love you now, I loved you then,
I love you for our future;
And we'll explore for evermore.
You'll be my guide and tutor.

In every way and every day
We'll be there for each other.
We thank you Lord in every way
Our new life to discover.

Geology

The course was called 'Geology'.
We've studied rocks and stone.
How Planet Earth was in its form
When pre-historic man was born.

We're going on a field trip.
Let's pack up all the gear.
The sun is shining and we're off
To lovely Notting-shire.

Not a moment to be lost,
There's so much to uncover.
The lovely church at Lowdham:
Is sandstone we discover.

To Epperstone, then Edingley,
But best we've saved till last:
The glorious Southwell Minster.
With time we've not surpassed.

Our churches are our heritage,
Designed with rocks and stone
With skills that time has never aged.
At last we headed home.

My Husband

You are my Rock of Ages
The one that I turn to.
My book has golden pages -
I'll save them all for you.

Some chapters are outrageous.
I've had my fun its true
And travelled all around the world
But ended up with YOU!

It's been a long and winding path,
With times full of confusion,
But with my Angel Guides to help
Love's come in a profusion.

So now it's Christmas time again,
We'll celebrate with pleasure
Life's golden pageant here for us
With memories to treasure.

Thank You for Sharing My World

Time is so precious
It cannot be bought
And sometimes we waste it
On much idle thought.
But I thank you for spending
This thought time with me,
To share my collection.
It is a reflection
And I hope call it poetry.

Goodbye and God Bless You!